Writer's Delight

Flairs and Glairs

Publication House

Disclaimer

This is a work of fiction and solely represent the thoughts of the corresponding authors of the articles. Our editors have tried their best to edit the content of all the authors and check the plagiarism.

All the write-ups in this book are unique and are only published in this book.

In case any plagiarism or error is found, only the author is responsible alone, and not the publisher or the Compilers.

Cover Designing and Book Formatting
Shubham Shah and Ishani Agarwal

Acknowledgements

The making of this Anthology would not have been possible without the co-authors.
I would like to thank one and all who trusted and inspired me to come up with new compilations. Heartly thanks to the co-authors for being a beautiful part in most hectic life.
Last but not the least, many many thanks to F&G publications for publishing this masterpiece and Miss. Surbhi Gupta for giving me the opportunity and her constant support till the completion of the project.

Co Author

Shubham Shah (Founder Flairs and Glairs)
Ishani Agarwal (Co-Founder Flairs and Glairs)

1. **Saloni Shah (Compiler)**
2. Surbhi Gupta (Project Head)
3. Priyanka Banerjee
4. Priyanka Dhull
5. Harshita Rai
6. Jackson Chang
7. Priti Darade
8. Vishakha Malukani
9. Amarpreet Kour
10. Rhythm Thakral
11. Deepu Bela
12. Janvi Sharma

Shubham Shah

(Founder- Flairs and Glairs)

Shubham Shah, an entrepreneur at "Flairs & Glairs" a brand with dynamics in events organizing and cultural educational pan INDIA, is a 26yrs old guy who recently has entered the digital platform of imprinting emotions. He has initiated with his own open mic platform to help budding poets and aspiring writers under his brand named as "Teekhe Zasbaaat"

He is a commerce graduate from the Bhagalpur City of Bihar. He states Writing has impersonated him since childhood and he has now been writing for over a decade!

Cooking, on the other hand, is his passion! He also mentions, trying out new things just tickles him!

When asked sir, Why SPICY EMOTIONS?

He smiled and added, "agar jasbaat teekhe na ho toh wo jasbaat kahan" Spices are all that blends! So do his words!

As a chef, he presents to you his dish! Hot and freshly served! Taste it! Feel it! Enjoy it! You can also find his writing in the Book "Teekhe Zasbaaat" and 50+ Co-authored anthologies. With his passion to explore opportunities across Platforms, he is working with keen devotion and We wish him all the very best for his future ventures.

He is Featured in the **International Magazine De-Mode** for his upcoming solo novel.

He is **Approved by Ne8x for its Lit Fest,** and is a **Golden Star Awards 2020 Winner.**

He is an **India Book of Records Holder** for his Anthology **Satrang,** and has the **Grandmaster** title by **Asia Book of Records**, for the same.

He has also been featured in **Prabhat Khabar**, **Dainik Jagran** and other renowned Newspaper for his achievements. He has also been awarded with **India Star Republic Award 2021.**

He has been a proud co-author to

India Book of Records (Title- Black)

World Book of Records (Title -15 Wonders of Poetries)

India Book of Records (Title - Aaina)

Vajra World Records Holder (Title - Gustakhi Maaf Hai)

High Range of Records Holder (Title - Gustakhi Maaf Hai)

Share your reviews on his

INSTAGRAM

       @spicy_emotions
       @shubham4shah

Or via email on

       shubham2shah@gmail.com

To stay tuned to his work and opportunities follow his business Handles

INSTAGRAM   FACEBOOK   YOUTUBE

       @flairsandglairs
       @teekhezasbaaat

WEBSITE:

       https://flairsandglairs.in/
       https://flairsandglairs.com/

Ishani Agarwal

(Co-Founder- Flairs and Glairs)

Ishani Agarwal hails from the City of Joy, Kolkata.
She is the co-founder of her Community "Teekhe Zasbaaat" and Flairs and Glairs Publication.
Been a Compiler for 45+ Anthologies, she is in the process for more. Co-authored in 150+ Anthologies. She is a India Book of Records Holder, a Vajra World Records Holder, a High Range of Records Holder and a Bravo Record holder.

Approved by Ne8x for its Lit Fest 2020, and Literary Icon 2020. Also a Golden Star Awards Winner 2020.

She has also been awarded with India Star Republic Award 2021.

She has been featured by the National Magazine "Taree Zameen Par" with the title 'unstoppable'.

Also featured in the International Magazine DeMode for her upcoming solo novel, she is proud to write on social issues, and is happy with the love she is receiving.

Connect with her on Instagram: @Ishani_agarwal_quotes / @compilations_so_far

SALONI SHAH
(Compiler)

Saloni, 19, is a quintessential poet with a fervent passion for all forms of art. A proud girl hailing from city Shrirampur, she is majoring in CS (AI) field. She started penning down poetry as a hobby. Most of her poetries are based on true feelings which she tries to express through words. Blooming as a budding writer she aspires to be a great author.

She has compiled 15+ anthologies out of which 1 anthology titled "Zodiac: A tale of 12 signs" is recognized and awarded by India Book of Records.

INFULA ATLANTIS

Droplets from the grey sky
Weakened my perception,
But the rumbling thunder
Was sturdy proof of its own deception.
Tales narrated in the past
Had been full of lies,
The glorious island of Atlantis
Was even more cosmic in size.
Was this a tranquil dream
Or one terrifying nightmare,
The mystical island of Atlantis
Could not be put to compare.
Sirens, angels what not I saw,
All against
This explainable course of law.
A man with wings
As dark as coal,
Whose silver eyes
Glanced through my soul.
Revealed to me the greatest fact
Of all,
After which I understood
Their judgement of fall.
Atlantis had not sunk
Beneath the ocean waves,
Instead it now lay
In celestial Eden's cave.

MOONLIT NIGHT

Today, under this moonlit night I sit still,

The wind caressing my face gently and feeling
something inside my heart differently.

A melancholic feeling in my heart tearing and ripping
my soul apart.

Some nights are made for torture
or for reflection or some for savoring loneliness and today my
heart surrounded by clouds of darkness.

I often think that the night is livelier than the day but
today acquainted with the night I lay.

The night has a world in itself, the moon embraced
by the clouds around, the pleasant night soothing my
weary mind and solitude is what I find sitting still under
this moonlit night.

THIS VOICE

I'm bounded by four grey walls.
They seem to have no end.
Something tells me that this place
Is meant for people almost dead.

Unlike the world I witnessed before,
This place seems oddly familiar.
Reading my mind, a voice informs:
"That's because you've always belonged here"

Should I be laughing?
Or am I supposed to cry?
Should I be feeling pain?
Should I be asking why?

The voice is heard again.
This time mocking my ignorance.
"You know the reason 'why',
Shed this mask of innocence."

I hate to admit this,
But that voice is perfectly right.
How can I be unaware,
When it's been etched into my mind.

The voice remains quiet for a minute.
Like it's watching some great show.
Trying not to miss the scene
Of a person falling to a mighty blow.

Oh, only if the person had known
That no one will come to pick them up,

To brush the dust off their clothes,
To hold them tight and say, "Well done!"

Just then one of the big grey walls
Turns into transparent glass.
On the other side of which is
The world glowing with an eccentric spark.

The same world I was once a part of
Until it decided to abandon me,
With things functioning better than ever,
People getting along with life easily.

"I'm sure you're not being missed,
Your presence didn't matter anyway,"
Snapping me out of my thoughts,
The voice finally decided to say.

"Who are you and where am I?"
I somehow manage to ask.
"You still have no idea, I see,
You're not as smart as you think you are."

"This voice that you've been hearing
Is one of the many inside your head.
It's had enough of being unheard,
It's crying out the things you left unsaid"

"The four big grey walls
That seem to never end
Is the prison you've locked yourself into.
Your lonely little cell."

A laugh escapes my mouth

While a tear rolls down my eye.
I need to be saved from myself
Before I end up losing my mind.
Loneliness can be deadly.
It's a numbing kind of pain.
It will leave you feeling empty,
And this voice will drive you insane.

This voice will drive you insane,
With a numbing kind of pain.
This voice will haunt you again.
This voice will haunt you again.

O POWERFUL GIRL

Stand up girl and walk another mile,
For you are strong and not fragile.

Have your say when people dismay,
They will have opinions, keep them at bay.

A friendly nudge or a was it a bad touch,
Be ruthless to thrash those who judge.

O powerful Girl, break that lock,
Your Character isn't decided by the ticking clock.

Your wardrobe is your own choice,
Shut them up who make a noise.

The time has come, to rule the throne,
The orthodox mindset will be mourned.

ANXIETY

Some nights are different, they hurt more,
My body runs hot and I lay on the cool floor.
Inside these four walls, I find myself a corner,
And I start sweating as my head gets warmer.

The pain starts in my chest, I hear pounding,
I lose track of my thoughts and my surrounding.
Maybe I'm being punished for having a weak brain,
It's more than I can handle, more than I can contain.

I try everything to distract myself and forget it all in the morning,
And when my eyes moisten, it's just a warning.
It feels like running out of air, like dying,
But it's just me being "over dramatic" and crying.

When anxiety attacks, everything is in vain,
And every morning I pray for it to never happen again.
But let me tell you this, it'll go away,
It's not a permanent disorder, it won't stay

POP CULTURE

When it is said that the only constant is the change,
Why can't we broaden our mind and also our range.

Why can't we upgrade ourselves, keep our thinking back,
Why can't we leave registers and move towards Mac.

It is also necessary to maintain our originality and to upgrade,
That doesn't mean our culture is going to degrade.

We need to leave our reasoning and behaviour Orthodox,
It's ok to do things which are out of the box.

Modernisation is necessary but option too,
We need to make evolution and a nation new.

It is important to adapt new things and also to create,
It is obvious to receive fame and also hate.

Today there are so many ways and so many door,
We can aspire and inspire generations more and more.

SURBHI GUPTA
(Project Head)

Surbhi Gupta, born and raised in Punjab, is currently a Law Student , B.Com honours graduate and an enthusiastic writer as well. She is also working as Project Head for Flairs And Glairs Publications. Having a Lawyer's mind and a writer's heart, her writings are sui generis, relatable, and inspiring. She has compiled 6 anthologies , co-authored in 40+ and currently working on 3 record aiming projects. Various achievements in academics , Legal events and writing platforms are feathers in her cap. Sight and smell of her own book someday is what she aspires to achieve as a writer.

Instagram Handle @surbhi_writes

A WRITER'S DELIGHT

A Writer's Delight lies truly in the words they write....

A friend, or our own family may at some point not able to understand the emotions accumulated in us, or situations we are going through, but we need to take them out or let them go. Cry or to rejoice moments, that only our heart understands.

A piece of paper and a pen will , like an ally, stay by our side, to store all our memories, moments you wish to never forget or you wish to share with somebody, but you cannot.

A Piece of paper and pen is just like magic akin to Hogwarts Pensieve in famous Harry Potter movies. Just like memories can be stored in pensieve and can be viewed anytime when desired, similarly, memories and feelings penned on a paper stays there forever and can be read anytime....

So if an apology unsaid to someone, but cannot be said now, write it down
If love never confessed, cannot be confessed now, write it down
If mistakes done cannot be undone now, write it down, because writing down won't make these things happen, but it will lift the burden off you beyond imagination.

A Piece of paper and pen,
with thousand thoughts attached
is waiting for you to befriend.

PRIYANKA BANERJEE

Priyanka , is an avid reader and an amateur writer. She belongs from West Bengal, India. She was a student of a vernacular school and was always passionate about teaching. She is an M.A in English and also completed her B.Ed. From her childhood she used to scribble a lot. Gradually all those scribblings turned into writings. She loves to write her heart out. Now she is a teacher of an English medium school. Besides being a teacher and a writer she is also an explorer .
She writes short stories, poems, micro tales and open letters and travel diaries. Many of her write-ups have already been published.

PART- 1
"SHE..."

Jiya was 21 years old and she lived in a mofussil area. Unlike her friends she was quite talkative and obstreperous. Jiya was perfectly contented with her life – her study, her family and her hobbies. She was the first member of her family who became a graduate. Everything was going well and Jiya was preparing herself for higher studies ; but her family thought that Jiya had studied enough and she should marry. Jiya was sitting near the window . She could see the green field where she used to play hide and seek with her friends in childhood. Suddenly her reverie was hindered by her mother's voice, "Jiya , are you ready my dear? They have come to see you. Open the door, let me see how my daughter is looking." Jiya opened the door; her mother was surprised; "Why are you not ready yet?" ,asked her mother angrily. "Ma ,why are you doing all these? I am not prepared for marriage. Please don't force me", requested Jiya. "Jiya , you are crossing your limit. Be ready and come downstairs," saying this Jiya's mother went downstairs. Jiya could not understand what she should do. Her saree and jewelleries were lying on the bed. Jiya stared at them for few minutes and went downstairs without being ready. "Namaskar aunty, namaskar uncle" – Jiya's parents looked back and saw that their daughter was standing there with folded hands . "Jiya, what is this? Why have you come here like this?", whispered her mother. "Just a minute Ma, I want to say something", said Jiya and continued , "Uncle , aunty I don't want to get married right now. I am sorry." An uneasy silence was there in the room. The boy's family stood up. "I didn't know these all are happening without your consent", told the boy's father and they left.

PART -2

"Okay grandma, I have to go now, call you later", saying this Jiya hung the phone up. That day, after arguing with her parents , when Jiya left her home she knew that the door of her house had been closed forever. With the help of one of her friends Jiya found a PG and started to stay there. After a couple of interviews she got a part time job also. She continued her study. After completing her study she got a job in a renowned company. It had been 3 years Jiya neither went to her house nor she talked with her parents. The only member with whom she was in touch was her grandmother. Jiya's father Mohan had lost his job as the factory where he worked , had been closed . They were helpless. "How can I run our family Ma?", asked Mohan with a drooping face. "Don't worry Mohan . God is with us." , replied Jiya's grandmother . She then went towards her ark and brought out some money and gave that to Mohan, "Keep it with you." "But Ma this is not a permanent solution. I need to find another job. I don't know what will happen", said Mohan. "Everything will be fine", replied the old woman with a smile. During the last four months the postmaster came and gave an envelope to Jiya's grandmother. Whenever Mohan asked about that , Jiya's grandmother used to smile. That day when the post master went away Jiya's mother, Nina asked, "Ma, as far as I know you don't have so much money that you could take the responsibility of the whole family; yet you have been giving us money for the last four months. Tell the truth Ma, where are you getting money from? What does the postmaster give you every month?" Jiya's grandma gave a one-sided smile and said, "Don't you think you should make amend?" "What are you saying Ma? Why should we make amend? What did we do?", asked Mohan. "Oh! Yes, you did nothing ; but your daughter did the right thing", replied Jiya's grandma. "I didn't understand Ma", said Nina. "Jiya knows about our condition and she sends

money every month . For her we all are still surviving", said the grandmother. There was a silence in the room . Jiya's parents' eyes were filled with tears. Silently they went away from the grandmother's room.

PART – 3

Jiya's phone was ringing continuously. Without noticing the number Jiya picked the phone up and said, "Hello." Within a second she recognised the voice of the opposite side, it was her mother's voice. Jiya's voice trembled. After 3 long years she talked to her mother. The door of her house had been opened again to receive her. It was a beautiful starry night. Jiya was lying beside her mother on the roof. She felt an inexpressible happiness. "Ma" Jiya whispered. "Yes" "I want to say you something" "What dear?" Jiya was silent for a few seconds. Then she said, "I have fulfilled my wish, now I am ready to fulfill your wish." With a smile Jiya's mother kissed her forehead and said , "May God bless you with all the happiness."

A QUEST FOR HEAVEN

Yasi was sitting outside of her house and unwinkingly she was watching the hill which was not far from her house. She heard from Kamala aunty that some children like her,stayed there. Yasi was thinking about her good old days when her grandfather took her for an evening walk; though that was not a perfect 'walk' for her, but her grandfather used to say "Yasi, let's have a walk together." Sitting alone on her wheel chair, Yasi was recollecting those stories which her grandfather used to say her. Yasi never saw her grandmother as she passed away before the birth of Yasi; but her grandfather used to say so many stories about his beloved wife that Yasi could visualize everything. Yasi's reverie broke by the voice of Kamala aunty. In the soft light Yasi saw that all the birds were going back to their nests. Every evening when she saw this ,she knew this was her time also to go to her room. Sighing Yasi turned her wheel chair. Every time she looked at the sky, a question came to her mind " Is there a real beautiful heaven beyond the sky?" Yasi was a girl of twenty-two. Her father was a well - known businessperson. Yasi got everything she needed, but somehow she was not happy from within. Her grandfather was her only friend in her family whom she had lost four years ago. Now there was no one to tell her stories or to take her for a walk in the evening. Yasi herself roamed here and there near her house. Kamala aunty was her only friend after the demise of her grandfather. From her childhood Yasi knew that she was different from her elder sister, Malini. Every time, in every occasion, she understood that Malini got more importance than her. Later she understood that the only difference between Malini and her was that Malini did not have to use a wheelchair to go here and there. Yasi's family never felt the importance of spending as much money for Yasi as they spent for Malini's education. Malini used to go to a well known

school, whereas Yasi was sent to another school where the school fees was less than half of Malini's school fees. Yasi never complained or wept for all these negligence; rather she thought all these quite natural as she was habituated with these since her childhood. The day when Malini went to London for her further studies, she saw that her father was bragging before one of their neighbours, " Yes, Mr. Roy, Malini is my quotable daughter . Let my daughter complete her M.B.A, then she will take the oar of my business." Yasi never heard this phrase-'my daughter'-from her father ,for her. It was Yasi's twenty third birthday; though she knew except Kamala aunty no one was there to wish her. Yasi had a hidden wish for a long time and the urge of fulfilling her wish was increasing day by day. Yasi was lying on the bed when Kamala aunty entered into her room with a big smile " Happy birthday Yasi, get up fast, today I will take you to the foot of that hill. A temple is there. Do you want to go there? It's been long you did not go for a walk, let's go today." After four long years Yasi again heard someone who offered her 'a walk' just as her grandfather. Yasi nodded her head and said, "Aunty I have a request." Kamala aunty was looking at her questioningly. "I want to go on the other side of the hill" Yasi kept on saying "I want to meet all those who are like me." Kamala aunty agreed. It was ten o' clock in the morning when Yasi reached the orphanage. There were many children- some were physically challenged and some were not. Yasi found six children who used wheel chair like her to go here and there. Yasi was amazed to see that there was no difference among those children. All were playing together; no one was neglected; everyone was treated equally; everyone was happy there. This was something which was beyond the imagination of Yasi. This was the first time when she started to think herself as equal as the other members of her family. She spent a good time there. She told the children some stories of kings and queens which was told to her by her grandfather. She also had her lunch with them – this was the first time she

was having lunch so happily as she never got a chance to sit with her family members during lunch or dinner time. In the evening she returned home. This was the first time she did not feel abandoned, this was the first time she felt herself as normal as the other people, this was the first time when she found a place where she got the treatment like a family member. Somehow she felt a strong connection with those children of that orphanage. Their innocent smiles were floating in front of her eyes. She started to go to the orphanage regularly and spent a good amount of time there. Gradually she started to go there without the help of Kamala aunty and spent more and more time with those children. The other members of the orphanage liked Yasi very much. Days passed. It had been almost a year Yasi was working in the orphanage as a teacher. She stayed there with the other members of the orphanage and rarely went to her house to meet with her parents. Kamala aunty often came to the orphanage to see Yasi. Yasi was twenty four. This year the whole orphanage celebrated Yasi's birthday with splendour. Of course Kamala aunty was present there, after all it was Kamala aunty who first brought Yasi into her heaven.

TOGETHER FOREVER

Who says we are kilometres apart? Let's catch the first ray of the sun together. Who says we don't talk regularly? Let's feel the moonlight together. Who says we can't touch each other? Let's close our eyes together. Ssshhhh!!! Can you hear something dear? Yes, the beating of our hearts. They are beating together. Oh! What a melody, what a tune, Nothing can be more beautiful.

PRIYANKA DHULL

Priyanka is currently a PGDM student at ABS Noida. She started writing when she was 8 and has been passionate about writing ever since. She expresses her feelings through her poems and stories and you can find a part of her in her pieces. She always wanted to make her father proud of her. It was her father's dream to see her work printed.

MOTHER AND CHILD

I opened my eyes,
Saw a beautiful face,
She was beauty
She was grace...

Her eyes were full of love,
Her pure soul shined through,
She was my mother,
Her expression so pure and true..

I am one month old now,
I see people around me,
But I have eyes for only her,
She gave me life, because of her only I am me...

I am 10 years old now,
I saw people cringe away from her,
Why are they scared of those beautiful scars?
She doesn't seem to care as long as we are together...

I am 20 now,
I know why, from her they pulled away,
She was an acid attack victim,
One scary incident that haunts her till today...

I don't care how she looks,
I don't care about those scars,
For me she will always remain,
The most beautiful woman I've met so far...

LUCID DREAM (A SHORT STORY)

I opened my eyes. I saw a white wall and I was lying on a white bed. It looked like a hospital room but more sweet smelling than medicinal smelling. I knew where I was. I've been here before. I was dreaming.

Unknown Voice- My dear child you've come again. Welcome.

Me- I... No... It's just a dream I'll wake up soon.

Unknown voice- (sadly) No my child, not this time.

Me- What do you mean? I've had this dream before. I've met you before. It was all a dream.

Unknown voice- Do you remember falling asleep?

Me- I... Uh... I am.. not sure... I was with my friend. We were at my house watching a movie. I am sure I fell asleep on the couch.

Unknown- No... You didn't... There was a fire at your house. You tried to escape but couldn't do it in time... You're dead.

Me- That's not possible... I...

But then I remembered smoke, heat and my friend screaming my name. Does that mean that they're telling the truth?

Me- But..but if it's true then where am I? I know I've been here before. I remember waking up after that and thinking it was all a dream.

Unknown voice-Yes, it was when you were little. You fell off the roof and were hospitalized. Doctors saved you but for a moment you lost your heartbeat and you came here.

Me- I remember my mother telling this story to my aunt. I almost died that day. So if I am dead, where am I?

A bright light filled the already bright room. It was blinding. Out of that, a beautiful woman materialized.

Woman- My child, you're finally home.

SOUND OF A QUIET CITY

It's too quiet now
Almost scary
The world has taken a bow
People are now wary

But although there're no vehicles
Or the loud noise of traffic outside
People are in their home like shackles
To laws trying and failing to abide

I hear the sound of a 6 weeks old baby
Who's not able to breath properly
Her this new life turned shabby
Just because people preferred fake faith than orderly

I hear the sound of the old mother
Who's fault only was to hug her son
Not knowing or caring to bother
But not able to see in her last moments her dear ones

I hear the sound of those doctors
Who leave their homes not knowing if they'll return
I wonder when they stand on their doors
Do they turn back and see on their family's faces that concern

I hear the sound of that Policeman
Who stands outside in danger for 12 hours straight
Urging the people to the safety of their homes
But still earning selfish people's hate
I hear the sound of that border police guy
Asking my father for masks or sanitizers
Because he doesn't have money or place or time to buy

But government is wasting money on people who are less than
wiser

I hear the sound of those hungry laborers
Whose kids are dying in their arms
But instead of being their caregivers
Some idiots are showering them with chemicals that harms

So tell me now it'll all be fine
There'll be end of this horrible pity
Because even though everything seems to be in line
I still hear the cries of this quiet city.

STRESS, DEPRESSION- YOUNG GENERATION'S FRUSTRATION

Let me recite a poetry of numbers
Statistics of who hung themself and who was a jumper
Failed in exam, got their heart broken,
Words from their families were left unspoken,

Out of 10000,
4000 were suffering from studies in school,
1000 were in college,
bullied by people who called themselves "cool"

2000 were those who married greedy men
Saw their father in pain, decided to quit instead then
1000 were those who were too much in debt
Trapped in tight corporate world's net.

The other 1000 were farmers
Who sowed more than they could reap
The last 1000 were those who were raped
Died to hide their pain too deep.

The sad part is these people were so young
Their dreams unfulfilled, their stories were left unsung
Just between 15-29, they suffered from stress and depression
Is there any way to end this young generation's frustration?

FAREWELL TO A BEST FRIEND

I'll remember you
Not because I knew you long,
Not because you proved me wrong,
Not because you made me cry
Not because you were so shy.
I'll remember you
Not because of how we worked
Not because of all your perks
Not because you're too polite
Not because of that one night
I'll remember you
Not because of how you complained
Not because of you always explained
Not because of "Can you please hold?"
Not because of how you were sometimes bold
The few reasons I WILL remember you..
Because of how always you made me laugh
No matter how life and situations were tough,
Because of how we talked all night
Telling each other truth and arguing who was right,
Because of how when you smiled with sparkled eyes
Made me trust in everything and feel the high skies,
Because of how you criticized everything about me
But me doing it myself you could'nt see
Because how I tore myself often and told you all,
About my every sad story, about my every fall...
So maybe it's a good bye
Maybe it's for best
But I'll remember you
In my heart for my life rest...

CHILD ABUSE - A NEVER ENDING CURSE

Half-finished art,
Crayons rolling on the floor
A 6 year old's crying
Screaming for help through the door

A 10 year old's new father came
Promising them a new start
A month later he became a monster
A man of urges, having indecent heart.

A 6 months old cries,
She doesn't know how to speak
The man doesn't even realise
What he's destroying is so fragile and weak.

A poor 5 year old is hungry
She asked for food from 3 men
They instead stripped her off of clothes
And gave in exchange 50₹ and a pen

These words might hurt you
You might hate me for this
But everyone needs to know the truth
About what happens during they're living in bliss.

HARSHITA RAI

Harshita is a commerce graduate and aspires a career in law .
She is a practicing writer and passionate about writing quotes
, poems and short stories. Being in a field and an educational
atmosphere of commerce and law , she spends a considerable
time writing journal , quotes and thoughts. She is more
inclined towards fictional writings , although she admires non
- fictional writeups too. She believes in the Art of living and ;
that the biggest power we have is that of " Humanity "

I AM WITH YOU

I may not be there in front of you ,
Doesn't mean I'm not with you.
I may not be holding you ,
Doesn't mean I can't feel you .
I want to obliterate your tears and ease your pain . For I know
, how gruelling it is for you. I may not be sharing your grief ,
Doesn't mean I am miserly and disregarding you . Have faith
, have patience .
For I know ; presence of almighty is real. We will meet soon
,
But only when the time is right .
And ; when you walk of the darkness ,
You'll find me unfurling the light.

SUNSHINE

Let the rays of sun conquer the shadows of
humiliation, anger, bad day, toxic people.
Let the rays, get absorbed completely in you. Let the rays,
bring new hope and dawn in your life. Let the rays, bring
that never ending brightness in your life, that'll enlighten
your soul and mind to infinity

" IT's OKAY "

It's okay to be honest.
It's okay to be ingenious,
to be kind towards others,
but remember never forget
yourself in this race.
Never forget that the kindness
you need to show in the first
place is to you; yourself. You
need not fight a battle inside
and make graveyard of things,
deep inside you.

" ENVIRONMENT "

Is there anything more mesmerizing than this?
The sunrise and sunsets.
The anatomy, that human's won't get.
That ombre in the sky,
That mild fragrant soil.
The green foliage and
The magnificent velvety sky.
This is the wonderland,
Where, birds could fly high.
Where, animals could stroll.
Yes! This is the synergy of earth.

LOST IN REALITY

Everything will be alright eventually.
But not all the time.
Sometimes, you'll put your soul on stake,
fight till the end but lose.
Sometimes, there's no choice; but to let go.
Remember, As far as you're willing to
fight, you are not a loser.
You tried, that's all.
The only control one can
have is self-control.
Know yourself, better each day.
Try to be calm as much as possible.
Remember, life is not a path full of
flowers and gems, which will enlighten
your soul.
This path is filled with rocks, stones and thorns
Every such thing that will make you
struggle and fight back

A COMMITMENT BEYOND LOVE

We'll forever be together;
Yet there will be spaces between us.
For, the breeze of love to flow
We'll always stand together;
In every twists and turns, highs and lows, but not too close;
For, the pillars of a home always stand apart, to safeguard it.
We'll always brew coffee for each
other; But not drink from the same cup
For, watching each other, while having every sip
in itself is wondrous.
We'll enjoy every bit of life, swaying and twirling together,
But at times we will let each other dance freely. For, the
strings of guitar are
even alone and separate;
But they create magic when played along.
We have already given our Heart's to each other;
but Nor for safekeeping neither In custody.
For, solely the almighty can do this,
we can merely treasure and feel it.
We'll always be a good listener To each other,
in good as well as in bad circumstances.
For, everything that makes sound isn't music.
At last, whether we are close or apart;
We'll forever be soulmates, until this era lasts.

TRIP DOWN MEMORY LANE

A trip down your memory lane, Is the
most astounding part of the day.
Your thoughts and presence;
Conquer me always.
Not for a minute or an hour,
For a lifetime.
In silence or in hustle,
I think of you.
All I do is cherish your
Memories and guard them
In name of you.
You were my inspiration
My idol, my teacher.
You gave me learnings for lifetime,
Your teachings serve as rule of thumb;
From which I will never part.
God has you in his home,
And I have you in my heart

JACKSON CHANG

Jackson Chang is an MA student enrolled in the English Program at the National Central University in Taiwan. He is interested in children's literature, poetry and translation. He has been writing poetry since 2018 and admires the work of Rabindranath Tagore, famous for his poems and songs, and for being the first Asian to win the Noble Prize in 1913.

SEA

The old man is sailing on the sea,
Looking at the seagulls flying above the seashore,

He recalls his memories to find something interesting,
A bunch of children is playing hide-and-seek at the coastline.

He hopes that his youth could come back again,
With his innocent smile and mind.

Nobody knows how deep the sea is,
Only the time can predict its depth and feelings.

Reflection on the surface is everyone's tear,
Waiting for someone to wipe up its scar.

WALK INTO YOUR HEART

Let me step into the warmth of your arms,
Let me bask in the sunshine of your smile,
Let me hold you a moment longer, my love.

I want to walk into your heart secretly,
With my sincere love and caring,
Roses are my symbols of true love.

I wish that you could follow with my steps,
Finding the sweet and bitterness through the love,
Until the time is frozen by your moment.

FARM

A lot of cattle and sheep are guided by their shepherds,
Who is singing the unique lyrics and rhythms on the farm?

The rhythms of Nature is the best melody on the fields,
The farmers are also grazing these beautiful places with their passion.

The breeze is secretly blowing the whole land away,
And the crops are swaying from side to side.

The scent of yellow wheat and dry hay is attracting my attention to recall my hometown,
Where lots of animals and plants are growing up with their steps and tempos.

O' my lovely farm,
I wish that you could be as pretty as a little girl,
With her innocent smiles to touch my heart!

PRITI DARADE

Priti Darade likes to read and write a lot. She always wanted to write something on her own, also likes to write poems and quotes.

ONE NIGHT

It was a Beautiful yet dark night with a growing silence every minute which was beautiful. I was crossing a small but attractive night café, it had a beautiful gate and its path was covered by green shrubs and fairy lights on them. On a snowy night, the cotton like snow flakes were falling on shrubs. Everything seems beautiful. I entered the little coffee café, chose a small table in the corner and there were very less people which actually made it calmer and more attractive. A thin, pale white waitress came near my table for the orders. "A tuna sandwich and a coffee with extra sugar will do, thank you " I said. She just bowed and went straight behind the corner. I looked around the place there were eight tables in fair distance, an aisle which goes from door to straight counter. Just three of them were occupied, one was by a couple they seemed like talking to each other and nothing around them matters, another table was occupied by a young guy who was working on his laptop. I was at last table. Well that's fair at 12:30 am you don't expect much crowd to be there. In all of these things one thing remains constant that the Dark silent nights is the most beautiful time in a 24 hours of madness. "Here comes your tuna sandwich and coffee" said Nancy. "Thank you" I said. Nancy's grandfather owns this café, she comes every year in winter in holidays and loves to help her grandfather in his café. Her father and grandfather doesn't get together well, so her father and family lives outside the city, but she loves her grandfather and visits him at any possible chance. "Its nice to see you Nancy" I said. "Nice to see you too Sarah , though this late….. what's the matter? "Nancy asked with a tensed tone. I looked at her and nodded to come and sit with me. She came and sat , cleaning her hands with the little white apron on a black skirt which looked beautiful with blue top. She was a tall and fair girl with brown hair. She is beautiful. "So what's the

deal" asked Nancy. Before I say something I looked around again the couple was at the second table and the handsome guy (which I assumed was handsome) was way ahead too. "Actually its been really weird these days" I said. "Why? What happened?" asked Nancy. "I think there's something unnatural happening with me from some time. I cant sleep, cant go alone anyway, it creeps me out . Things starts to move by itself sometimes and etc. I am not able to figure this out, what's going on with me " I told her with little tension in my voice. "Did something happened near your apartment or near" asked nancy "None that I can remember" said I after thinking for a while. "Why don't we go and look near or about your apartment?" She asked while standing up with little enthusiastic expression. "I don't know. I think it would be easier to just move to another place" I suggested. "Are you sure its going to get fine after that? I think we should go." Nancy insisted. I grabbed my coat and bag, put the money on the table for the food I didn't even touched. We started walking after a while Nancy speeded up and was ahead of me. She became awfully quiet since we left the café. "Listen! Do you think it a good idea" I said in a little loud voice as she was ahead of me, looking in a car window mirror I thought I was looking beautiful in black dress and blue coat with black boots. "Hey! Do you think it's a good idea?". I asked again. "Its going to be fine. Keep walking." She said. I was little scared and tensed as she was ridiculously quiet again and the street was deserted but then I saw an old couple walking across the road. It felt good. Then she suddenly took a wrong turn. "We are going on a wrong turn Nan." I almost shouted. "She didn't seem to listen me." "Hey are you listening……" I stopped, something was wrong I noticed that this street has so many lights that shadows are big and bright. But…There was only one….I looked at Nancy, she was still walking but she didn't have a shadow. I turned around and ran until I didn't reach the café. I burst barged in went straight to another waitress. "Is..is

Nnnancy alright?" I asked her while trying to catch a breath. She looked puzzle and asked "Yes I think she is. Why would you ask?" I stammered a little "I..I..I don't know. I am sorry but can I talk to her?" I said. she looked at me confusingly. "She didn't come this year." Were the words of waitress. I was sweating, my mouth felt dry it was impossible to understand whats going on. I was not in thinking state anymore I decided to call my uncle so that he can pick me. We left café in some time. The very next day I woke up, (I stayed at my uncle's apartment) and turned on the television. I was astonished it was unbelievable but maybe it explained what happened last night. The building where I had an apartment was on the news. The news said that new neighbors the husband and wife who recently moved in were found dead. I remembered the first time I had a talk with her. She told me about her husband and the way he used to torture her. I promised her to help as soon as I get back from the work trip I have to go on. As per doctors the wife was murdered by husband the very next day, and husband committed suicide yesterday, the day I got back. "It was her, it was her it was her" I said and kept repeating until I got back to my senses. She wanted my help to take revenge like I promised her. *After 3 months* I've been living in my apartment again, I assumed she got the help she wanted. Nothing strange happened afterwards. Though I don't think I'll ever forget this incident.

NOBODY KNOWS

At the end of the day
I am always alone at the bay
Thinking of the moments of joy
Figuring what went wrong, oh boy!

After all these failing years
I've left with no one who cares
Every day seems same
As if its saying end the game.

I've been trying for success
But its not easy coz we r over with recess
I can witness my mournful downfall
All i can ask is why me of all.

We all started together this journey
Then why some are happy and other in only worry.
My dreams arent as big as their's
But yes i can say i m the one who bears

All i expected was little joy and
All i got,...just closer to being mad.
They say,the more you wait the slow it comes
The only thing i saw coming were heart burns.

I everyday wakes up and sleep to same circumstances
What i really want is to be there ur importance announces.

VISHAKHA MALUKANI(MORIKA)

Vishakha Malukani belongs to Indore. She loves reading & writing. She started writing when she was in 7th standard. She being an introvert soul finds writing the best way of expressing feelings. She is the greatest devotee of Lord Krishna that's why her pen name is Morika. She has worked with TCS Gujarat. She is a published author. She wants to become psychologist.

FROM THE DIARY OF AN INTROVERT SOUL

This story is about two opposites, one was caring, calm, lovable, innocent & an introvert whereas the other one was bold, bindaas, friendly & an extrovert.

You might have heard opposites attract but does this happen in "real" life or its just about "reel" life in bollywood romantic movies? Exciting isn't it??

I will tell you everything in detail. How they met? How they fell for each other? Was it that easy for them? Was that actually a love or temporary attraction? How their families reacted? And lot more questions. Everything I will tell you.

Be ready to listen to this story …

Story focuses on 2 main characters

Kreesha

Aarav

Let's begin

Like other normal days, this was a different day in Kreesha & Aarav's life. Let's see what happened.

14/JANUARY/2014 TUESDAY

Kreesha was scrolling through instagram and than she checked follow requests list deleted the ones who were totally unknown and was checking the profile of the ones who had mutual friends. She being an introvert soul never accepted follow requests of strangers. Then she saw it was Aarav Bansal. His smile was so attractive .Kreesha checked his profile and saw her cousin being friends with Aarav. She accepted his follow request at 9:45pm approx. & at 10:10pm he texted her Hey! Thanks a lot. Kreesha hesitated and just replied a smile emoji.

The chat continued for 1 hour of formal talks. That day they didn't talk much still she was happy because at first she felt some connectivity. It was really a beautiful feeling Kreesha was an introvert girl & was never comfortable with boys but with Aarav things were different.

15/JANUARY/2014 WEDNESDAY

Aarav messaged Kreesha "Hie, goodmorning cutie" (she was blushing) someone first time called her cutie
(Compliments from opposite gender are always magical. Isn't it..?)
(Ahhann.. these feelings can't be penned down into words)
She replied "Hello gdmorning".
He instantly came online and replied "I miss you na yarr kaha the tum itna time lagta h reply krne me"
(it all felt like a dream to Kreesha because before this she never interacted with a boy. She can't stop blushing she felt loved. They both had already fallen in love its just none of them confessed)
She replied : "Abhi aayi just college se. I am sorry" and then there conversation continued for 3-4 long hours.

Everything was going on so smoothly. They were getting closer with each passing day. They shared every secret with each other. Aarav was in 3 relationships before Kreesha. For Kreesha he was the first. Feelings were so different as we all know.
(Again words can't tell what Kreesha was feeling)
नया नया सा नशा नए नए प्यार का
Hayyeee …

14/FEBRUARY/2014   FRIDAY

Aarav proposed her at 11:55pm

Aarav : Krishu baby I don't know what you will say, how you will react but all I want to say is I Love You a lot. Will you be my valentine sweetie?

(She wanted to say Yes eagerly she was waiting for this moment & finally when the moment came she hesitated because she had a complex about her dark complexion).

बाकी तो लड़की के मन में लड्डू फुट रहे थे !!

Kreesha: "You look so good I don't deserve you I am not compatible with you"

Aarav : Ssshhh… shutup don't you ever dare to say anything wrong about my krishu baby, I fell for your soul & I mean it. You are the purest soul I have ever been with. What is in looks baby, they fade with age but beauty of soul is a permanent thing & is irreplaceable. So just keep shut & say yes and be mine forever and who the fuck said you look ugly you are the most beautiful girl on this planet for me & that is what matters. Right jaan..??

She was not convinced, still their conversation continued till morning 4:30am & finally she said "YES" things were now different between them. They had some soul to soul connection since the day one but as Kreesha was always uncomfortable with boys, Aarav came as a blessing to her who changed her mentality about boys, that not all boys are same not everyone falls for perfect figure & fair complexion, there exist boys who fall for inner beauty. Aarav always motivated Kreesha to fall in love with herself first and with anyone else later. This was the best thing about Aarav.

Everything was going on so well. Kreesha was so in love with Aarav that she started writing & trust me her words are love. I

am one of the biggest fan of her words that's why sharing her story with you. She is an inspiration.

20/MARCH/2014   THURSDAY

Now the day came when Aarav asked Kreesha for taking their relationship to the another level. Kreesha again hesitated. But it was again so easy for Aarav to convince her. She agreed. That night they were completely lost into each other. There bodies and soul were seduced. They made love whole night under the blanket over the call.
The night ended real soon it was morning 5:30am still none of them wished to disconnect the call.
(As this was the only medium for them to get connected)
(I swear its not that easy to be in a long distance relationship it takes a lot of patience, dedication & sacrifice)

30/MARCH/2014   SUNDAY

Now they both decided to take one more step in their relationship and talk to their parents. But before that it was important to be capable of taking each other's stand. Aarav wanted to be capable enough to ensure Kreesha's parents that her future is safe with him. That's why they both mutually decided to focus on their goals for the betterment of future.

Aarav wanted to become an Engineer and Kreesha wanted to publish her own book and to set up her center as a Child Counsellor.

It was really difficult for them. They gradually stopped talking if one feels weak without talking the other one stands stronger. (Trust me it's never easy to stop talking to someone you are addicted to no matter it was long distance but there was

nothing like a distance because their morning started and day ended with each other)

It's been 2 years to the day since they stopped talking. Aarav and Kreesha only talked occasionally with each other, in between this span of time their parents started searching partners for Aarav & Kreesha as they both were 22 now. But still they had a long way to go. Here Aarav told his parents about Kreesha but she hadn't yet told anything because she was waiting for the right time. It was their 2nd year, Aarav had 2 more years to his studies as he was pursuing Engineering & Kreesha had 1 one year as she was pursuing BA in psychology.

2 YEARS LATER

18/MARCH/2016 FRIDAY

They both had a conversation like they used to have before they chatted for hours, talked over the call and couldn't stop themselves from getting emotional. They decided to make love whole night as they both badly missed each other & 2 years was not a less time ofcourse.

1:20am it was they were completely lost into each other, they relived all those beautiful moments over the call under the blanket. Suddenly Kreesha's alarm rang it was morning 5:25 she daily wakes up to study. That day she didn't study, for her all that mattered was Aarav. They poured out everything they had been hiding, controlling their feelings since last 2 years. Aarav even told her how he had told his parents that its Kreesha whom he will marry.

(Kreesha felt the luckiest girl on this planet she used to stay away from boys she never knew someone from distance can

love her so so much. People who say long distance doesn't works, this story is for them)

Again they both had to be strong and take decision of not talking for coming 2 years because this was really crucial time for both of them. For both of their internship & job so that they have to struggle less to convince their families. This time they decided to not to talk even on occasions. Kreesha disagreed but Aarav somehow convinced her, they both decided to switch of their mobile phones so that they both wont get distracted.

(it was so difficult for them to spend every minute without each other but for their future's betterment they did)

As both of their phones were switched off if anyone of them even try but couldn't connect.

4/APRIL/2016 MONDAY

Kreesha's parents found someone who was best compatible for her according to them.This rishta came via their common relative. He was 3 years elder to her working in Pune as a Software Engineer. His name was Tarun he saw her in his cousin's wedding and fell for her innocence but he was waiting for the correct time to send her the proposal.

Lot many discussions were going on in Kreesha's family, things were almost finalized according to her parents. Tarun and his family were to visit Kreesha's home for Roka Ceremony.
Here Kreesha couldn't connect with Aarav. She told everything to her mother,she scolded her saying "Keep your

mouth shut, you will have to do what we say, don't even think of him, he's from another caste. How dare you think that. We will file a police complaint against him that he is forcing you to talk to him and his future will be spoiled, better you say Yes."

Tarun and his family arrived
He already liked her so from his side there was nothing to be discussed. Kreesha was asked if she wants to ask anything she said "NO". Things were finalized they touched feet of their elder ones and were asked to go visit temple for the new beginnings. They both went for a long drive, visited temple & Tarun purchased a dress for Kreesha for their Roka Ceremony that was to be held the same evening. Tarun tried a lot to talk to Kreesha but she wasn't responding properly. They exchanged their numbers but Kreesha used to avoid his calls most of the times. Tarun thought she might be busy or uncomfortable because of Arranged rishta.

(Kreesha still couldn't connect with Aarav, one month had already passed to her Roka Ceremony)

5/MAY/2016   SUNDAY

Kreesha's father was checking Tarun's facebook profile and he found "In a Relationship with Aastha " which he updated a week before which means after their Roka Ceremony. Her father called Tarun's father and cancelled the engagement. He came home angrily, Kreesha thought Tarun might have told his father that she is not talking to him properly. She was so much scared but the exact opposite happened, he hugged her tight and said he was sorry. She couldn't understand what was happening, her mother asked him what happened? He told them everything and also told that he said NO to Tarun's family without giving any explaination.

(Kreesha felt happiest at that moment).

She locked herself in room, felt both good as well as bad for herself ,she thanked God.

Same day at evening 7:15 Aarav called as some relations just need soul to soul connection. Aarav said "Babe sorry I couldn't control myself I was getting so much negative vibes, are you alright sweetheart?".

Kreesha started crying and told him everything. They both together cried and Aarav said now he will not leave her alone ever and they decided to talk till the time Kreesha get out of this trauma. They started talking regularly spending hours together but this time hours were fixed 1hour morning, 1 hour noon, 1 hour evening and 1.5 hour night. This schedule continued for a week then Kreesha stood strong for both of them and said "Aaru baby now I am completely fine lets now again focus on our future".

"Bhaad me jaaye future baby tum hi ho jo ho I won't leave you ever, abhi thoda time durr kiya toh kya se kya hogya jaan".

Kreesha was a strong girl, she convinced Aarav to focus on himself for now.

They both again mentally prepared themselves to stay away from each other to focus more on future to convince their parents for their marriage.

They both started working more harder to achieve their goals & to be each others forever.

18/DECEMBER/2016 THURSDAY

Aarav got placed in "Infosys" he wanted Kreesha to be the first one to know this good news. He called her on her landline number, fortunately she received the call, he gave her the good news and she was on the cloud nine that day. But for her there

was more struggle waiting. It was a day which calls for huge celebration but they postponed their happiness and planned to celebrate later together.

Few Months Later**

Kreesha's book got published. She started working in an NGO for getting experience to set up her own NGO. Everyone was so happy with her now was the time that she can take her and Aarav's relations stand. Her parents were so happy and proud of her. She told her father everything about Aarav and insisted to get married to him and ensured that she will be happy with him. Her father didn't said Yes neither he said No, he just kissed her forehead and left. It was so late. Next day Kreesha called Aarav to tell everything. He asked her "Krishu jaan tumne papa ko bata diya hai kya hmare bare me"
She said "Jaana aapko kaise pata chala". He said "bass awei jaan ". Then they changed the topic.

(2hours later Kreesha's father came back home & asked Kreesha to dial Aarav's number in between these 2 hours he enquired about Aarav from her cousin being mutual friends with them) she dialed his number & handed over her phone to her father.

"Beta when are you talking to your parents about our Krishu and your relation" (Kreesha's father)
(With a exciting & nervous tone Aarav replied)

Jii…Jii Uncle whenever you say, we will come tomorrow if you say.
"Beta papa bolne ki aadat daal lo ab"(Kreesha's father)
Like this their conversation continued for 10-15 mins, they finally decided to meet on 14/Februay/2017 on their 3rd year anniversary to get "Rokafied".
(They both could not ask for anything else to God. Long distance doesn't work, people say, but not always. Its all about

how much you individually are capable of holding onto, no matter what comes your way)

14/FEBRUARY/2017FRIDAY

They met for the first time ,that also for the promise of lifetime togetherness and with the happiness and blessings of their families. They were lost into each others eyes. Their eyes reflected their happiness. So much happiness all around. Same day they called the *pandit* to decide their marriage date. Pandit gave 3 dates 6june, 10june & 18june. Aarav's birthdate is 18 so they decided it to be 18/June(their present feelings cant be penned down in words right now).

"Finally a big day arrived" Kreesha was dolled up like a princess & Aarav looked a royal prince. They both took oaths together ,saat pheras around the agni. Kreesha was happy as well as sad for leaving her parents forever.

Everything is going on so perfectly by God's grace.

10/JANUARY/2019 WEDNESDAY

They are parents of cute little angel named MISHIKA. Kreesha has her own NGO in which Aarav & Kreesha work together. Aarav manages both so well, his job & the NGO.

Blessedfamily
Happyfamily

AMARPREET KOUR

Amimmy, desired to be known by this name, 20 years old, the author through her writings intends to bring the traces of ongoing love of her life. She in this collection of poem, profoundly, describe her strong desire with her love, whom she is destined to meet.

THE DAY I WILL MEET YOU:-

I am eagerly waiting for the day I will meet you,
the day of our union.
This love prospering soul is waiting for her love sufficient
soul.
My dear! come meet me, bring me the most wished day, even
though it's my last day.
Just bring this day to me, my love.
Year's of wait, dry tears of countless nights, mythical smiles
of countless mornings, now needs to be put to an end, that too
be only by you.
My love, draw me to this day, while my eyes are still able to
see the sun and the moon and the stars and you.
Listen! I have made my preparations, the day I will meet you,
I will be the brightest star of the sky, like a gleaming drop of
rain, I will come to you, cuddle you tightly and tightly and will
get blend with you.
Dear, allow me to nuzzle you as this is my exclusively chance.
You told me, everyone needs to be loved and to love, but my
beat of heart, I am telling you I am going to only love you,
today and forever and this is my vow.

THE DAY OF OUR LOVE

Cloudless bright day,
cloudy, rumble will work much better.
The nature approving two souls,
desperate of union,
unknown of their love, or maybe known,
only nature or they themselves know it.
One soul with the yearning eyes for the sight of others, the
other soul with an eagerness for the peek to the appearance of
another soul.
Oh! the minute is here,
the standstill of time is here,
see the anguish of both, see the discursive eyes of both.
Like the moon grazing the water,
two of them cuddled each other,
two of them snuggled each other,
the ebb has been formed,
the ebb of sensation,
the ebb of love has been formed.
The day has come, the day of the union has arrived.
The day of falling in love and accepting love has come.
The day to be loved and to love has come.

THE DAY I WILL GIVE THE FIRST KISS TO YOU

Traditional is my idea,
heedful is my nature,
I have a craving,
I have a yearning,
I have a hunger,
To kiss you, to touch your lips with mine,
I know I can't do it, but,
Still, the fascination in me urged me to:-
The touch of your skin,
the warmth of your face,
the redness of your husk,
the trepidation of mine,
the stiff sweat of my skin,
the numbness of my limbs,
the touch of your skin,
everything is dreamed by me,
A dream of open eyes,
a dream to be fulfilled with my close eyes,
I am ready and asking you to get ready,
Here I am with you,
To give you my first kiss, only when you permit me,
I am waiting and will wait if you want.

THE DAY I WILL FEED YOU:-

Tired of chewing special,
I have something very modest,
tired of eating by the option of others,
I have something choice only by you,
tired of eating the flavour of others' hand,
I have something, l, tasted by my hands,
tired of eating by the excellent, I have something made by the clumsy,
tired of eating just for the sake of eating,
I have something not just for the sake of eating,
not so outstanding I think, but for sure favourite of yours,
The first time of my try
here I am presenting you,
Don't know whether you like it or not,
but my love just feel it,
feel the love I put,
feel the hands that feed you,
feel me in it,
I am waiting for the day when I will feed you with my own love, my own taste of yours.

THE DAY I WILL HOLD YOUR HAND

Let's go for a stride,
let's go for the chatter,
far in the lumber,
or maybe far beside the mist,
In the quiet twilight,
Dark and sparkling,
Away from the clatter
away from the flashes,
just you and me,
just two essences of us,
let's talk my love, anything you like, anything you wish,
but I have a plea,
I have an impulse,
I have an illusion,
'with the talk, I want the touch',
That not so fragile hands of yours, with not so skinny hands of
mine,
fingers intertwined like the vine quagmire with the veneer,
just you and me, I want the first moment to touch your hand,
I want my first moment of touching your heart.
The shy, long wanted day, I want to hold your hand today and
forever.

THE DAY I WILL GET DRUNK WITH YOU:-

The day I am procrastinating most eagerly,
the night I am loitering most eagerly,
the juncture I will lay my trust to you,
Yes! you read it right,
My dear! I trust you the most,
not just for my protection, but, for my choices, for my morality,
too easy to say, but hard to believe,
but I trust you the my most accessible and resistant states,
too you I want to be the weakest and toughest woman,
I need your protection, and, I intend to protect you,
when I will be drunk, I want you to listen,
I want you to hear my words,
indiscretions I know they will be, but true to you, I will guarantee,
just the day I will sit and sip with you,
I will be me and I want you to be you, the true you,
I am eagerly waiting for this day.

THE DAY WE WILL BE TOGETHER

Although a utopian I sound,
an inefficacious person I sound,
but with my every whiff,
with my every scene,
with my every moment of life, I am dwelling,
I imagine togetherness of us,
I imagine you and me altogether,
I imagine you and me to be us,
I imagine you to accept me,
I imagine myself to accept you, although I have done it already,
there is no space for others when we are together,
there is no guilt in thinking, even when I do it without shimmering.
The desire I have, the intention I carve,
the words I create, the scenes I create,
everything in it is related to you,
everything of it is created by me only for you,
to fall in love is nobody's choice, but to maintain the love,
It is a want we have as a choice,
I imagine the day we will be together,
I imagine the night, I listen to your heartbeat, running along with mine,
I imagine the morning, where I will see you first, lying next to me,
The sip of coffee,
the sound of birds,
the breeze of woods,
the crackling of leaves and a beautiful garden,
I imagine all these to be experienced by you.

THE DAY YOU WILL SAY ' I LOVE YOU' TO ME:-

This is the day I wait for the most,
this is the day I want the most,
the day which will be the fortune of my life,
the day you got to unlock your heart to me,
there are times, I said, I love you to you,
but there is not even a minute where you said to be the same
with all your heart,
I know it's hard, but not unthinkable,
The love between us is unspecified, yet it is inferred to both of
us,
the togetherness is impossible, yet I speculate it to be possible,
I am waiting for the stop of time,
I am waiting for the song of your tongue,
I am waiting for the whispers of your mouth,
I am waiting for the words " I love you."
I am waiting for the day when you will say "I love you" to me
on your own will.

RHYTHM THAKRAL

उलझे ख़्वाबों मे ज़िद का थोड़ा स्वाद हूँ ।
सब गगन मे कैद है, मैं पिंजरे मे आज़ाद हूँ ।।

Rhythm Thakral born and raised in a small town Saharanpur which is in UP. Rhythm considers her faith and family most important to her. If she is not with her friends and family you will find her in her favorite corner reading books. Being an only child Rhythm found companionship in the fictional characters. Her love for reading credit goes to her mother. Rhythm says,"My muma always says that, people will not guide you to the correct path but books will !". Her father says that "she got this habit of reading from her grandfather". Rhythm's love for reading led her to the similar education atmosphere. After pursuing graduation and post graduation in English Literature, she is now a teacher in a well reputed English medium school.

Rhythm is a budding writer and has keen interest in dark literature and likes to write twoliners, stories and poetries.

She is a co-author of a book named "Ikhtiyaar".

Rhythm believes that "Books don't reflect what a writer writes but it reflects what a reader reads"

GOLDEN CAGE

Dear diary,

  Oh I missed you sooo much. I haven't talked to anyone since ages . Finally found you ,there is a lot to tell you. Last we talked when I was about to get married. Can't forget that day! Was looking forward to spend blissful journey with love of my life. It was such a beautiful day," ma baba were so happy" It's been a long time I hadn't talked to them. I hope God's gracious hand is on them! I hope they miss me. "I miss them".
Nevermind....
Few days back.. my husband brought a little birdie. I had never seen such a beautiful bird in my life.
As soon as she entered our garden it's chirp broke the silence of the house. It was such a beautiful sound.
Our garden was covered with yellow cage. The birdie was looking at it and chirping day and night. I don't know why it was doing like that , it's her house now. She would get all the food and love she desired then why? why ? she was looking out of the cage?
That birdie was a Scarlet tangerine, it was as bright as blood.
Its sable pinions were as dark as a pall.
She resembled me and I resembled her.
I also have that scarlet color !
Sometimes it is on my head, Sometimes on my waste, legs, chest. Wherever his belt touches me I get that scarlet color.
Today I have it in my hands!
The birdie is out of the cage!....

QUOTE

She is the Sun,I'm the moon.
Sometimes we coexist,
Rest of the time we wait for another eclipse.

किताबों में गुम हो जाने की कला भी अनोखी है,
आज भी लोग दुनिया को दुनिया की नज़र से नहीं देखना चाहते।
-

You are like a Book to Me,
I always find Solace in you.

DEEPU BELA

Dr. Deepu N Bela hails from Jam khirasara a small village in dev bhoomi dwarka district. A distinctive personality who is an ambivert by nature. She is a sophisticated writer who works consistently to give a spark to her valuable thoughts. Writing for her is a way of expression herself. Her writeups are published in many Anthologies and magazines too. She is a physiotherapist. She believes in Miracles. "I paint the canvas of mind with pretty colors that fly"

कहानी किसान की..!!!

में जगत का तात
कहता हूं जोड़ के दोनों हाथ..!
कहता हूं अपनी कहानी
भर के इन आंखों में पानी
मेरा दर्द सबने है जाना
फिर भी ना जाने क्यों है सबसे अनजाना.!

कहलाता तो हूं मैं; "जगत का तात"
फिर भी ना जाने क्यों हूं हर पल अनाथ
क्यों नहीं सुनता कोई मेरी अरदास!

वैसे तो हूं मैं"अन्नदाता"..
फिर भी तरसता हूं दो वक़्त की रोटी को
मेरा ही पैदा किया हुआ धान
में ही खरीदता हूं चुका के दुगने दाम!

वैसे तो ....
"जय जवान, जय किसान, जय विज्ञान"
कहता है पूरा हिन्दुस्तान..!

जवान की शहादत पर
शोक मानता है पूरा हिंदुस्तान
नवाजा जाता है दे के वीरचक्र का सम्मान!

विज्ञान की तरक्की पर
नाचता है पूरा हिंदुस्तान
नवाजा जाता है दे के पुरस्कार!

जब जब ये धरती बंजर हुई
जैसे लगा हो दिल पर खंजर कोई
नहीं बरसा एक बूंद भी पानी
मिट्टी में मिल गई मेरी जिंदगानी
ब्याज के बोझ तले डुबके
थक हार के मौत को गले से लगाई!

मेरी मौत पर कहां था ये हिंदुस्तान?
क्यों नहीं की किसी ने मेरी दरकार?
क्यों नहीं सुनी किसी ने मेरी पुकार?
क्यों मैं नहीं किसी पुरस्कार और सहायता का हकदार?

जिंदगी की किताब..!!

जिंदगी है यादों की वो सुनहरी किताब...
हर पन्ने की अपनी कहानी, अपने किस्से..
हर पन्ने पर अपनो के वो हिस्से...
कुछ खट्टे तो कुछ मिठे वो नग्मे...

कहीं अपनो का प्यार
कहीं सपनों का वो संसार
कहीं गैरों की वफायें
कहीं अपनो का यूँ साथ छोड़ना

कहीं सपनों का यूं टूटना
कहीं अपनों का रूठना
कहीं खुशियों का जूम के आना
कहीं गम से आहें भरना

कहीं सपनों का यूं सच होना
कहीं अनचाही खुशियों का मिलना
कहीं टुटके बिखर जाना
कहीं गिर के फिर उठना

कहीं पहले प्यार का नया उमंग
कहीं दिल टूटने का वो बेहद गम
कहीं दोस्तों से तकरार
तो कहीं तकरार के बाद का प्यार

हर पन्ने पर बदलते रास्ते और मंजिल
नहीं बदला तो सिर्फ मंजिल पाने की चाहत,

टुटके फिर उठने का वो होंसला,
खुद पे यकीन और कुछ पाने की जिद्द,
आगे बढ़ने का वो जज्बा।

हमने जो की थी मोहब्बत...!!

हमने जो कि थी महोब्बत वो आज भी है।
माना है अधूरी हमारी कहानी पर
इन निगाहों में मुकम्मल होने की
ख़्वाहिश आज भी है

तुम ने जो दिया था वो गुलाब आज भी है
माना मुरझा गया है वो पर
किताब के पन्नों में उसकी महक
आज भी है।

हमने जो किये थे जो साथ रहने के
वादे आज भी है
माना आज हम साथ नहीं पर
यादों की वो लड़ी में हम साथ आज भी है।

तुम्हारा वो रुला के फिर हँसाने का
सिलसिला आज भी है
माना अब हँसी एक सपने जैसी है पर
डायरी के हर पन्ने पर आंसूओं का
अक्स आज भी है।
वो तुम्हारा बालों को सहलाना और
माथे को चूमना आज भी है
माना अब तू दूर ही सही पर
इन हवाओं में तेरे होने का
अहसास आज भी है

वो तुम्हारा कहना फिर आऊंगा
मिलने वो आज भी है
माना अब तू नहीं आएगा पर
दिल को तेरा इंतज़ार आज भी है।

बन बैठे है..!!

कल तक जो थे अजनबी
वो आज नबी बन बैठे हैं।
कल तक जिसका अक्स तक नहीं मौजूद था
वो आज दिल में बनके छवी बैठे हैं।
कल तक जो ख्वाब भी ना थे
वो आज हकीकत बन बैठे हैं।
कल तक हम जिसे ढूंढ़ते थे चांद सितारों में
आज वो हमारे जमीं आसमान बन बैठे हैं।
कल तक जिस से थी मीलों की दूरी
वो आज हर सांस पे जरुरी बन बैठे हैं
कल तक जो थे गुमनाम
वो आज हम-नाम बन बैठे हैं।
कल तक हमें जिसकी कमी थी
आज वो इन आंखों के अमी बन बैठे हैं।
कल तक जो महज एक किस्सा भी ना थे
वो आज पूरी कहानी बन बैठे हैं।
कल तक ना था कोई रिश्ता
वो आज फरिश्ता बन बैठे हैं।
और हम, जो कल तक थे बेजुबां
वो आज शायर बन बैठे है।

तेरी याद..!!

तेरी याद कुछ ऐसे आती है
जैसे बंसत में पानखर,
बिन मौसम बारिश आंखों से बरसाती है।
वैसे तो हर मौसम के होते है चार मास,
पर तेरी यादों के मौसम के है बारमास।

कभी दिन में सपने दिखाती है तो
कभी पूरी रात जगाती है तेरी याद,
कभी दुनिया से मुझे जोड़ जाती है तो
कभी भीड़ में भी तन्हा छोड़ जाती है तेरी याद,

कभी यादों में है फ़रियाद तो
कभी फरियादों में भी है तेरी याद,
क्या सिर्फ मुझे ही तड़पाती है तेरी याद?
या फिर तुझे भी रुलाती है मेरी याद?
अब तो इंतजार है की तेरी याद
तुझे कब लाती है??

कहानी बेवा की..!!

तेरे जाने से कुछ मर सी गईथी में
उस टूटी चूड़ियों की तरह
कुछ बिखर सी गई थी मैं।

जिस सिंदूर को शोख से सजाती थी मैं अपनी मांग में
आज उसी लाल रंग को छूने के भी काबिल नहीं मैं
तेरी दी वो चूड़ियां शोख से पहन के
कैसे तुझ को दिखाती थी मैं
अब सुनी कलाइयों में खुद को छुपाती हूं मैं।

याद है मुझे तुम कहते थे...
"तेरे होने से ही मेरी जिंदगी में ये सारे रंग है"
अब तो होली में भी खुद को छुपाती हूं
आंसूओं में खुद को डुबोती हूं।

तुम थे तब तेरी पसन्द के रंग पहनती थी
अब तू नहीं तो मेरी पसन्द के रंग भी नसीब नहीं
तुम्हें शिकायत रहती थी ना मुझसे..
मैं सजने संवरने में घंटों लगाती हूं
अब घंटों तेरी यादों में गंवाती हूं।

मेरे तो सारे रंग तो गए तेरे संग
अब जिंदगी हो गई है बेरंग
अब बस मेरा एक ही रंग
जिस पे ना लगे कोई रंग

अब तो आँख के आँसू भी सूख गए
ख़तम हो गए खुद को बहलाने के बहाने

बस रह गए है तो लोगो के ताने
ना जाने क्यूं सब मनहूस ही मुझ को माने
गलती से लग जाए कोई रंग
याद दिलाते है सब मुझे तेरे जाने का ग़म

मेरे लिए तू तो मर के भी ना मर सका
पर तेरे जाते ही लोगो ने
मुझे जीते जी ही मार दिया..!

JANVI SHARMA

Janvi Sharma is just 10th pass out , She started writing poetry because she could really connect with music especially with English emotional music ......by listening to the music she got ideas to write a poetry ..and her work has also been published in two Anthologies.

DON'T BE ESCAPED

Escaping is not a solution People will forget you If you wouldn't resemble your appearance Most escape Because they don't want to Accept their failure, Most of them get depressed Because they don't get what they want Before dying think of your parents, Think of your mother who cares for you And went through so much pain To bring you into this wonderful world Dont beg for those relationships That don't even belong to you, Don't escape, cherish your present Cherish your each and every moment Because the life you are living, Someone is dreaming to have the same life.

KEEPER

I am the keeper,
Of your untold tears ,
Of your untold secrets,
Of your untold happiness ,
Of your untold loneliness,

Now I see the same eyes,
With some kind of betrayal,
With some kind of guiltiness,
I'm the keeper of your unkept promises,
Being a keeper is disguise......

QUOTE

People say if there is a battle between heart and mind, always choose heart

But if heartbreaks, then we always run back to mind ......

Don't allow anyone to break your heart ....

QUOTE

If society says why this person becomes devil....
Don't ask me why I became devil..,
Ask yourself what you have done with me......

QUOTE

If someone wants to make you down .... Don't feel bad .... It is because you are always above them.... Be happy and be positive

Flairs and Glairs, a platform by a student for the students. We are esteemed youth struggling to carve out our path for our future and we follow a basic mindset Since everyone is not born with all-round skills. Joining hands with people who are born to execute it with perfection is the best way to evolve. Self-Evolution is the need of the hour but, evolving as a community is what we strive for. The initiative as kickstarted by, Founder- Mr. Shubham Shah with the motive to utilize the skillset and talent of writing has now a team of 10+ people who are actively participating into newer forms of learning and discovering talents among youngsters. We Provide platform and services like Publishing opportunities, Open mics, Workshops, Hands-on training. Operating with Brand Name of Flairs and Glairs (Publication House), we offer the chance of elevating a passionate writer to an esteemed author With Brand name Teekhe Zasbaaat. We bring to you an opportunity to get accustomed with the Public Speaking and Presenting of Thoughts along with regular challenges to brush up your inking spirit. The newest initiative to extend our services we introduced in a new writing Platform- The Glittering Fables and Ink Over Tears.

We Choose to Fly Like A Falcon than to be a Leg Pulling Crab.

To Know More: Infoline – 7781900870
Mail Us At-
flairsandglairs@gmail.com / info@flairsandglairs.in
Or Visit is at
www.flairsandglairs.com / www.flairsandglairs.in
Social Handles- @flairsandglairs @teekhezasbaaat